FATE
OR FOE

Also by Alexandria Blaelock

SHORT STORY COLLECTIONS
The Histories of Hayward Hall
Lovelorn, Lovestruck and Love at First Sight
Common or Garden Variety Heroes
Case Files of the Wilkinson Detective Agency
Unavoidable Fates
Christmas Travesties
Five Faces of Felicia Clarke
Little Place Called Home
Security Directorate Dossiers v. 1.
Security Directorate Dossiers v. 2.

FICTION
That Love Nonsense
Taipan vs Brown
The Ghost and Ms Cox
Friends Like That
Weaving the Wildwood
Wolf vs Orb

MS BLAELOCK'S BOOKS
Stress Free Dinner Parties
Signature Wardrobe Planning
Holistic Personal Finance
Minimally Viable Housekeeping
Planning a Life Worth Living

PICTURE BOOKS
Australia Felix

SELECTED SHORT STORIES
Alma's Grace
Blood and Bloody Profanity
Cancelled by the Cartel
Dingo Hunting
Honoris Virilis Respectu
Mince Pie Mystery
Remains of Christmas

FATE OR FOE

A FATES SHORT STORY

ALEXANDRIA BLAELOCK

BlueMere Books
MELBOURNE, AUSTRALIA

BlueMere Books
quirky & unexpected

FATE OR FOE

Dierdre paced around the edges of the randomly coloured and patterned carpet that sat in the centre of the wooden floor of her room as she contemplated the nature of fate.

Her fate in particular.

Her seemingly unavoidable fate.

For one thing, her name was Deirdre. The broken-hearted.

What kind of irresponsible parent would gift that name to a child - no matter how influential the namesake.

As a second thing, her parents had found an "advantageous" match for her, and she was being shipped off to another country to marry a stranger.

Leaving everything she knew behind.

So, to be completely honest, not all that advantageous to her.

The advantageous match in question had not bothered to introduce himself to her, either in person or by letter.

Clearly, he had no regard, and precious little concern for her, so how exactly was that advantageous to her?

And if that wasn't bad enough, her parents were trying to convince her he'd seen her at a party (when she wasn't permitted to go anywhere), and had fallen in love with her, and was too shy to reach out to her.

Did they think she was an idiot?

Real-life did not consist of fairy tale endings.

As if to mock her, a pair of brightly coloured birds swooped past her tower window, calling sweet nothings to each other. Seemingly intent on the Spring mating season.

This new match was certainly nowhere near as advantageous as Ethan, for example, who was very concerned with her health and welfare.

So much so she'd been charmed and snuck out of the manor to spend generous amounts of alone time with him in the forest.

So much time she'd gone way passed charmed, bypassing infatuated, straight to falling in love with, and wanting to run away from her responsibilities with him.

Though it had to be said, he was a lot less keen on her now she was betrothed to another.

You had to wonder whether he had actually liked her at all.

For a third, she was stuck in her bedroom.

Not exactly forbidden to leave, but with guards posted on the outside, presumably to protect what was now a *valuable* asset, certainly not allowed to roam as freely as she had before the betrothal.

It wasn't a particular hardship; it was a nice enough room as far as rooms go. She paused to list its positives as if she was trying to sell it:

A spacious ten by twelve paces.

Bright and well-lit, with several small embrasures.

Airy, yet cosy.

Easily defensible.

Pristine white walls and ceiling that bounced the light around.

Plenty of books to amuse herself with when she didn't want to do any needlecraft.

Which was always, causing no end of trouble with the state of her hand-stitched trousseau.

And her mother's nerves.

Deirdre's younger sister Cara (the beloved) would have traded places with her in an instant.

They'd done their best to persuade their parents, but to no avail.

For some ridiculous reason or another, the advantageous match required the eldest daughter, not the younger.

Or any other daughter should there be more than two.

Not to mention that tradition described the marriages from eldest to youngest, with Cara remaining at home forever to take care of her parents while their eldest brother ran amok being the local laird.

In so many ways, a tragic turn of events for *all* involved parties.

Though, in theory, not her problem.

Anymore.

Deirdre took another lap of the carpet.

Cara was propped on Deirdre's bed, examining her red hair for split ends, snipping them off with a tiny pair of scissors attached to her châtelaine.

Now and again, she gave in and peeled one back, trying to get it the length of the strand.

"I've heard there's a place you can go to beg the Fates to change it," she said idly.

Deirdre took five paces, and flung herself on the bed at the opposite end to her sister.

Who was hogging the pillows and presumably leaving splinters of hair there as well.

"And?" she said.

Cara paused, lock of hair in one hand and scis-sors in the other, looking at her sister. She shrugged, "that's all I know."

Deirdre slapped Cara's closest leg to her, "you would have to be the most useless person I know."

"It's a shame mother doesn't feel that way."

Cara dropped the trimmed hair and sectioned out another lock. "I don't know what you're complaining about anyway. I'd do about anything to get out of here."

"I know," Deirdre groaned, "we *all* know."

Too restless to settle, she picked herself up and started pacing again, "who told you about this place where the Fates receive petitioners?"

"I overheard the laundry maids gossiping. Apparently, they have a shop. Somewhere in town. I think they said it was a tapestry shop."

"And what are their fees?"

Cara shrugged again, "I don't know. Proportional I guess. Depending on what fate you're trying to avoid, and what you're willing to accept instead."

Deirdre bent down, trying to look in Cara's eyes, "you do realise this is almost the exact answer to our problems?"

"'Spose."

Deirdre growled impatiently, "I despair of you, really I do. We could have been rid of this, and you haven't even prepared an escape route."

"I don't need to," she screwed her face into a mocking, smiling mask, "you're so desperate you'll do it for me."

And that was true.

Cara did nothing.

Ever.

Beloved by name, and utterly charming when she wanted something.

No one was immune.

Beloved she might be, but utterly ruthless in getting anything that took her fancy.

Leaving a trail of carnage in her wake; the corpse of a puppy she'd coveted, the burn-scarred face of a love rival, and the boy who'd been besotted with the burned face had mysteriously fallen from the tower.

Deirdre asked all the laundry maids until she found out where the Fate's shop was.

Though in the end, she had to say Cara want-ed to know because *everyone* knew how she felt about her life.

And everyone thought Deirdre couldn't be an-ything less than over the moon happy that some guy (who she was sure had never seen her) should be so in love with her that nothing would satisfy him but that she marry him with haste.

And yeah, sure, she was living the fairy tale.

But.

She wanted a *real* life.

On her own terms.

According to the maids, the shop was in an-other city, about half a day's ride away.

She didn't expect she'd be coming home, but for a plausible excuse, she'd have to stay away overnight.

And that excuse would have to be reputable.

She could go shopping, but there wasn't any kind of industry in the city that might attract a Lady.

Or visit a shrine to pray and purify herself for the marriage. Assuming there was one there.

And that was another thing that bothered her about the marriage.

Despite the tradition of marrying in the bride's home town, he'd demanded she travel to his. Without her family.

Or a bridal procession.

In fact, he'd sent a squad of armed guards to fetch her.

Though it didn't altogether matter whether there was a shine or not.

If she said there was one, her mother would believe her.

Because Deirdre had always taken her responsibilities seriously.

Always done what she was told.

And always confessed when she had done something to disappoint them.

Nonetheless, she quizzed the laundry maids further and discovered that there was a shrine.

Even better, for the goddess Áine - goddess of love, wealth and Summer.

Handy.

Deirdre knew she'd have to sacrifice her honesty at some point, but didn't want to have to lie any more than she had to.

She couldn't sit comfortably with it.

At least not yet.

So that was the first plan. To boldly seek permission to travel to the next city to receive a blessing. She shuddered just thinking about it,

Then squared her shoulders, and stood tall, spine straight; failing that, sneak out.

But much easier if she could go openly.

The next issue was how she might be able to slip away from her guards.

Presumably, she'd need a woman's excuse. Some kind of ritual where men weren't welcome.

She continued her enquiries.

And it happened there *was* a Druidic community nearby that could offer a pretext for some alone time. Though how to get from there to the tapestry shop was another question.

Or even where the tapestry shop was.

With the date of departure rapidly closing in, she had no real choice but to just get on with it.

Telling her parents turned out to be no trouble.

Going away for a night of ritual purification was fine with them, as long as she took her sister along with her.

And came back ready, and willing to stop with the sad face and miserable attitude, and travel to her new husband without further delay or complaint.

Slipping the guards was nowhere near as easy.

The guards sent with her were not those she'd grown up with, prepared to let her get away with a modicum of misbehaviour, but those her husband-to-be had sent.

Any shred of humanity concealed by their warlike armour and closed helmets.

Always assuming they were actually human.

After being denied entry to the community, they set up camp insultingly close to the boundaries. So close, they were right up against the hedging that surrounded it.

And her sister, as her only attendant, was no help whatsoever.

"I can't wait to see what you do next."

It was so tempting to leave her behind.

In the end, she sacrificed her honesty and stole some servant's clothes from the washing line.

And then her hair, hacking it off after a slight hesitation, so she looked like a boy.

A boy with a clean, soft face wouldn't do at all, so she rubbed ash on her cheeks and chin to disguise that.

Deirdre knew it would be worth it.

And if there were no fates, and she couldn't make a deal, then hopefully she'd get far enough away before her betrothed's guards got suspicious about the delay.

A maximum of 24 hours on foot.

How long did it take a horse to gallop that far?

Or could she hide in plain sight - did the guards know what she looked like, or did they just see the outward trappings?

Better to pray to each and every deity that the Fates existed, *and* were willing to make a deal.

Sacrificing her dignity she dressed in the boy's clothes, then sacrificed her poise, fruitlessly begging her sister to dress in the servant's clothes.

Then begging her to leave via the mendicant's gap in the hedge.

But Cara's dignity would only be satisfied by walking out the front door.

So Deirdre sacrificed even her status, following Cara as if she was her sister's servant.

She kept her eyes on the ground as the guards attempted to stop Cara, who pointed out they had nothing to do with her and her shopping plans.

Reminding them their duty lay with Deirdre, who was safely inside observing the marriage blessing rituals.

They grumbled suspiciously, but in the end, they had no real choice but to let her, and the "boy" leave.

Deirdre followed her meekly, allowing her to walk several paces ahead.

Mostly for the show of it, and only a little so she was forced to control her temper.

Even when Cara slowed to allow her to catch up, Deirdre slowed as well to remain a few paces behind her.

Cara found the tapestry shop, and Deirdre had the idea she'd known where it was all along.

Three women were sitting on a long bench outside the store.

The youngest, whose strawberry blond hair hung loosely around her shoulders declaring her to be a maiden, wore a red dress.

She was holding a piece of fine embroidery in her lap, the needle pushed through a corner so it didn't get lost.

The dark-haired woman's face was sun worn. She wore a wimple and a black dress, suggesting a widow. She was flicking a measuring stick around the fingers of one hand.

The final woman was wearing her white hair in a crown of plaits around her head, and a spotless white gown. She radiated a sense of eternity but looked about the same age as the red-haired woman. She was sharpening a pair of shears.

"I demand to see the Fates," said Cara.

The women didn't acknowledge her. The red-headed woman leaned to her right, and the black and white-haired women to the left, looking around Cara at Deirdre.

Deirdre knew they were judging her, and as she was sincere in her desire to seek their favour, she bowed deeply.

They looked at each other for a moment, then the white-haired woman stood up and walked into the store.

Cara attempted to follow her, but Deirdre held her back until the others had followed the white-haired woman in.

Only then did she drop her arm, allowing Cara to go in.

As Deirdre entered the store, she felt a kind of flicker. As though somehow, the interior they entered was not attached to the facade.

Or perhaps somewhere else entirely.

The room inside was lighter than she expected, and she saw no end to it.

A tapestry hung along the wall on her left, a seething mix of threads that wouldn't let her eyes settle on any one point.

As she looked along the tapestry, which seemed to stretch further that the endless room, she could almost make sense of it.

She heard something like a bird flutter, and looked up to see hundreds, if not thousands of small glowing tapestries hanging from the ceiling.

It reminded her a little of the Great Hall at home, the banners of the knights, both dead and alive, suspended from the beams.

While they did not glow, the suspended tapestries were obviously the source of the light. Deirdre had no idea how, or why, they were glowing.

Cara was right behind the women as they walked further into the space, but Deirdre stopped every few paces to look at the racks of different coloured threads dripping into the enormous vats of dye.

She tripped over an uneven flagstone and realised they'd started talking and she hadn't noticed.

She hurried to catch up.

The redheaded woman turned to Cara and asked, "what is it you want?"

"I want to be Deirdre," she said, almost before the woman had finished speaking.

"Cara!" Deirdre roared, though she couldn't have said whether she was more shocked by her impudence, or that she was too dense to come up with something of her own; preferring to take Dierdre's life.

As if it was as easy as changing her gown.

"What?" Cara put her hands on her hips, the classic tell she was preparing for a fight. "If you get your way, you won't be here.

"And if you get your way, then I'll get what I want."

It was true that Cara had always wanted what-ever Deirdre had, but to hear her say out loud, that she wanted your life, was another thing en-tirely.

Still, Cara was right.

And Deirdre had no right to be so mean-spir-ited about it. She should allow herself to be glad; Cara might be happier that way.

She straightened her shoulders and looked at the woman. "Fine, I'm prepared to walk away from it all."

Cara smiled like a cat with cream; not that Deir-dre had ever seen a cat smile, cream or no cream.

As she watched, Cara just faded away, as if she had never been born.

And technically she hadn't.

"What will happen to Cara now?"

"You have no need to know," the white-haired one said.

The black-haired one tutted, "No need for that Agatha." Taking Deirdre's arm, she drew her across to a vat of blue dye and waved her hand over the surface.

Deirdre leaned over the surface to see.

《《 • 》》

Deirdre paced around the edges of the random colour patterned carpet that sat in the centre of the wooden floor of her room as she contemplat-ed the nature of fate.

Broken-hearted by name.

Broken-hearted by nature.

Being shipped off to marry a stranger who hadn't even sent a letter for her with the proposal

Stuck in her bedroom without so much as a younger sister to help pass the time...

《《 • 》》

"Well that's not going to end well," said Aga-tha.

Deirdre grabbed her arm, "what do you mean?"

"It's not your fate anymore, why do you care?"

"I don't want Cara to get hurt.

Agatha smiled a straight lipped smile, "you heard her, she said she wanted to be you."

"But—"

"Not the eldest daughter, or your replacement, but you. *Specifically,* you."

And then she turned to the black-haired woman, "though I fear I've messed things up a little for you."

"Well, you *were* a little cruel. Anyway, it's nothing much. I can make it work."

"So what happens when someone wants to be them, and the original wants to be themselves?" Deirdre asked.

"Same thing as will happen to you," the redhead said, walking across to the vat, "we find them new, unoccupied circumstances and erase their memories as we go."

"Then I won't remember being me?"

"No one does dear," said the black-haired woman, "we don't leave any lingering regrets.

"Now, what do we do about you? What kind of life are you looking for?" said the white-haired woman.

"You're asking me?"

"Of course dear," said the black-haired woman, "what's the point otherwise."

"Oh," Deirdre said blushing, "I thought you'd just look me over and assign something."

The women looked at each other.

The white-haired woman snorted, and the redhead turned away, her shoulders shaking. The black-haired woman chuckled, turning it to a laugh and couldn't stop.

The redhead couldn't contain it and started laughing, and set the white-haired one off too.

She clutched Deirdre's shoulder, and as if it was a virus, she was laughing too.

With no idea why.

Eventually, the women got a hold of themselves.

"Ah that was good," said the white-haired one sighing.

The black-haired one rubbed her sides, "I haven't laughed like that in centuries."

The redhead was still trying to catch her breath.

"What did I say?"

"Most people," said the white-haired one gasping, "have a very definite idea before they get here."

"Ah. I thought that would be presumptuous of me."

And that started them off again.

While they laughed, Deirdre started thinking about what kind of life she wanted, and by the time they stopped had prepared a list.

"Okay then. I want to be someone ordinary," the women looked away from each other.

"And I want to love and be loved. Marry someone who sees me as an equal partner. To make a difference."

"That's quite a wish list, but I think we can manage it," the redhead said.

The women linked hands, and the air shimmered.

As the room faded around Deirdre, she thought she might have heard one say "you know she's going to die anyway, right?"

And another reply, "yes, but this time it'll mean something."

The scene rushing toward her was terrifying.

《《 • 》》

A city street, full of mirrored towers that filled the sky. It was loud, *really* loud, and she felt the brightness of the lights must surely burn through her eyeballs and singe her brain.

A line of men in black uniforms were arrayed before her. They carried almost imperceptible shields on one arm and held nasty looking black cudgels in the other.

She wasn't sure who they were, but they had the look of seasoned warriors. Something about the way they carried themselves; firm, yet light on their feet.

The air was thick with smoke, and some weird and metallic smell within it was making her gag.

She was hot, packed in a large crowd of sweat-soaked people, jostling around her.

"Gilda," someone cried, "Gilda snap out of it. The cops are coming."

Gilda shook herself and squared her shoulders. "I'm here to demonstrate my democratic right to peacefully protest. The only way those thugs are going to get me out, is in a body bag."

THE END

As a small token of my thanks for reading...

Please enjoy 10% off everything (excluding shipping)

at alexandriablaelock.com

with the code deirdreten.

Turn the page for some ideas where to use it,

Life interrupted

To say the letter was a surprise was an understatement. It arrived addressed to Miss Finlay Cox, which made the contents even more extraordinary.

Orphan Finn Cox inherits a cottage. Thinks it holds the key to her origins. Of course she takes a look. Who wouldn't?

But when she gets there, she gets more than she bargained for.

Is it friend, family or foe?

All she wants is a place of her own.

When Alison Porter finds a tiny cottage for sale, she thinks her dreams have come true. Inside virgin bushland, "Crow Cottage" sits on the smallest parcel of cleared land.

It's old. It's run down. It's keeping a secret.

Stumbling through a mysterious portal in the garden, she finds herself in a place of mystery and intrigue. As the past, present and future collide, she must unravel the secret, for only then can she reweave the tapestry of time.

If you love a story of twists and turns, where nothing is what it seems, grab Weaving the Wildwood today

Meet Morag Clementine. The new housekeeper at historic Hayward Hall.

Her practical and capable attitude usually keeps her out of trouble.

bove all, her no-nonsense, get it done approach. And her get in the middle of the scrum outlook. Just as well, because Hayward Hall needs someone like her.

In this genre-spanning collection of original stories, Morag finds herself ensnared in the History of Hayward Hall...

No ordinary housekeeper, can Morag save the house, one century at a time?

Perhaps you'll carry your new books
in one of these bags

Enjoy them while drinking from
one of these mugs

Or wearing one of these t-shirts

ABOUT THE AUTHOR

Australian author Alexandria Blaelock writes mostly fantasy and mystery.

She's appeared in the Stringybark Anthology *Crowd Surfing*, *Pulphouse Fiction Magazine*, and *Ellery Queen's Mystery Magazine*.

She's also written five self-help books applying business techniques to personal matters like getting dressed, tidying up, and feeding friends.

When not exploring parallel universes, she talks to animals, indulges in K-dramas, and sips Campari. She lives in the Dandenongs, where she relishes the sound of birdsong, the scent of gum leaves and the sun on her face.

Discover more at https://alexandriablaelock.com.

www.ingramcontent.com/pod-product-compliance
Lightning Source LLC
Chambersburg PA
CBHW051829180726
48283CB00004BA/1369